親戚及相關的字 Relatives & Related Characters

Chinese U See

4.

Min Guo
郭敏

起步版 Beginner's Edition

U0130559

香港字藝出版社
Hong Kong Word Art Press

| Chinese U See 4 | *Beginner's Edition* | Relatives & Related Characters |

Author: Min Guo
Illustrator: Min Guo
Editor: Kim Yueng NG
Publisher: Hong Kong Word Art Press
Address: Unit 503, 5/F, Tower 2, Lippo Center, 89 Queensway, Admiralty, HK
Website: www.wordart.com.hk
Edition: Second edition in Hong Kong in July, 2017
Size: 210 mm×190mm
ISBN: 978-988-14915-6-5

| 象形卡通 4 | 起步版 | 親戚及相關的字 |

作　　者： 郭　敏
繪　　畫： 郭　敏
編　　輯： 吳劍楊
出　　版： 香港字藝出版社
地　　址： 香港金鐘金鐘道 89 號力寶中心第 2 座 5 樓 503 室
網　　頁： www.wordart.com.hk
版　　次： 2017 年 7 月香港第二版
規　　格： 210 mm x190 mm
國際書號： 978-988-14915-6-5

哪一種方法更有效？

象形卡通　　　現代漢字　　　一般圖畫

　　　象形卡通以生動的生活畫面，增強了識字教學的直觀性、形象性和趣味性，能夠使學生在輕鬆愉快的氛圍中立刻辨明漢字的字義、字形和筆畫，能有效地提高學生的識字能力和速度。象形漢字是小小的藍圖，象形卡通就是它們的設計圖像，把漢字轉變成圖畫的過程，是培養孩子觀察力、想像力和創作力的最佳方法。

　　　象形卡通是根據現代漢字的字形、字義、筆畫、結構、文化內涵、字與字之間的關聯，并參照有關歷史文獻、甲骨文殘余的象形字、民間傳說、風俗習慣及地方方言等所創作的。象形卡通也是根據對現代漢字象形特點的研究、現代六書、現代漢字字理的研究和兒童認知理論所設計的。

Which Way Is Better?

Pictographic Cartoon	Chinese Character	Common Picture

ròu

meat

Pictographic cartoons add straightforward, lifelike, and interesting elements to character recognition, help students understand the meanings, the shapes and the strokes of Chinese characters immediately, efficiently improve students' ability and speed to recognize these characters in a fun way. They also support an easy learning environment for Chinese education. Chinese pictographs are little blueprints: the pictographic cartoons are their designed images.The process of changing characters into pictures is the best method to develop students' abilities of analysis, imagination and creativity.

Pictographic cartoons are created based on the shapes, the meanings, the strokes, the structures, and the connections of modern Chinese characters, referring to the related historical research and documentation, cultural connotations hidden in the structures of modern Chinese characters, ancient pictographs, folklore, customs, and local dialects. They are also designed based on more than 10 years' research on the pictographic characteristics, the Six Formations, the explanations of modern Chinese characters and the theories of children's cognitive development.

Table of Contents
目錄

The Stroke Orders 筆順

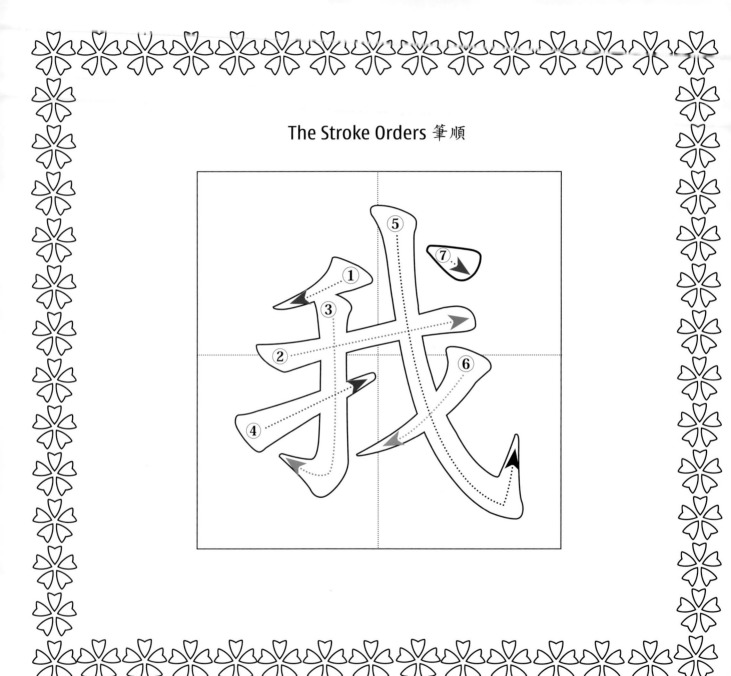

Lesson One 第一課

我

I/me

Wǒ shì Xiǎoé

我 是 小 娥 。

I am Xiao'e.

7

The Stroke Orders 筆順

她

she/her

Tā shì shuí
她是誰*？
Who is she?

*誰有兩個發音〔shuí〕和〔shéi〕前者比較正式一些。

The Stroke Orders 筆順

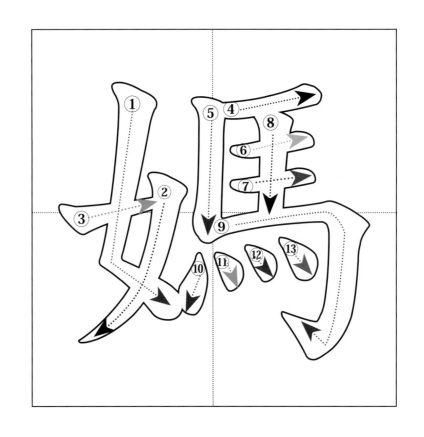

mā

mother

Tā shì wǒ mā ma

她是我媽媽。

She is my mother.

5

The Stroke Orders 筆順

tā

他

he/him

Tā shì wǒ bà ba
他 是 我 爸 爸 。
He is my father.

The Stroke Orders 筆順

tā

你

you

Nǐ hǎo， nǐ shì shuí

你 好 ， 你 是 誰 ？

Hello, who are you?

yé

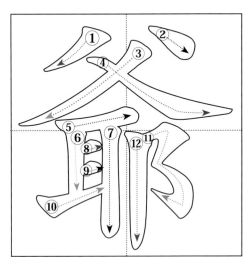

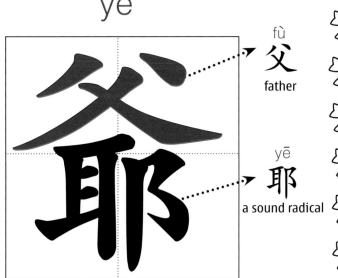

fù
父
father

yē
耶
a sound radical

grandfather
(on one's father's side)

tā　shì　wǒ　yé　　ye
他是我爺爺。
He is my grandfather.

shéi/shuí

who

Tā shì shuí
1. 她是誰？
Who is she?

Tā shì shuí
2. 他是誰？
Who is he?

Wǒ shì shuí
3. 我是誰？
Who am I?

The Stroke Orders 筆順

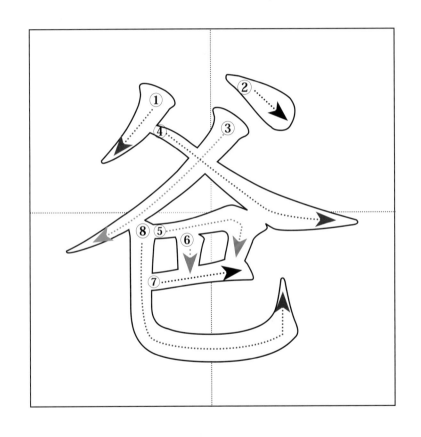

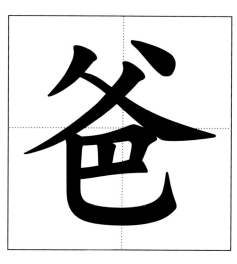

bà

爸

father

Tā bú shì wǒ bà ba

他不是我爸爸。

He is not my father.

The Stroke Orders 筆順

nǎi

奶

grandmother/milk

Nǎi nai shì bà ba de mā ma

奶奶是爸爸的媽媽。

奶奶 is my father's mother.

The Stroke Orders 筆順

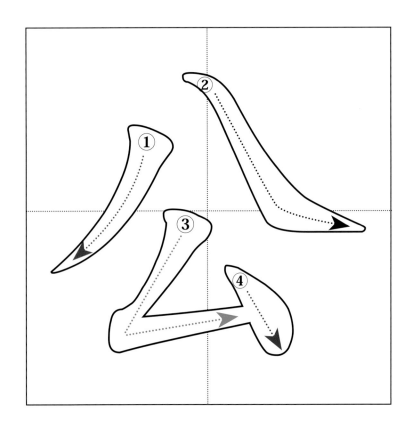

gōng

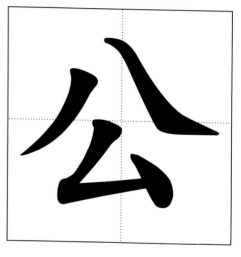

male/public

Wài gōng shì mā ma de bà ba

外公是媽媽的爸爸。

外公 **is my mother's father.**

17

The Stroke Orders 筆順

pó

old lady

Wài pó shì mā ma de mā ma

外婆是媽媽的媽媽。

外婆 is my mother's mother.

19

The Stroke Orders 筆順

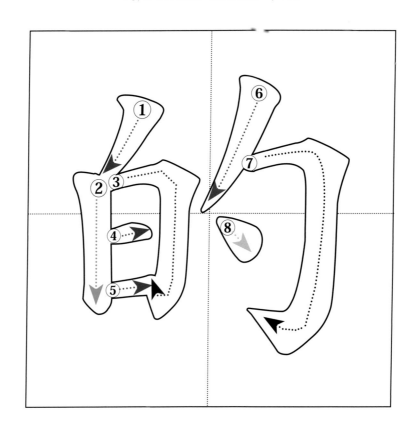

de

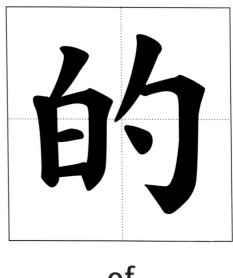

的

of

Bái cài zuò de tāng
白菜做的湯。
The soup is made of cabbage.

21

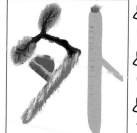

lǎo	ye
姥	爺

grandfather

lǎo	lao
姥	姥

grandmother

fù	qin
父	親

father (formal)

mǔ	qin
母	親

mother (formal)

Match the characters with the cartoons.
字畫相配。

牠 她 他 你 媽 嗎 我 找

The Stroke Orders 筆順

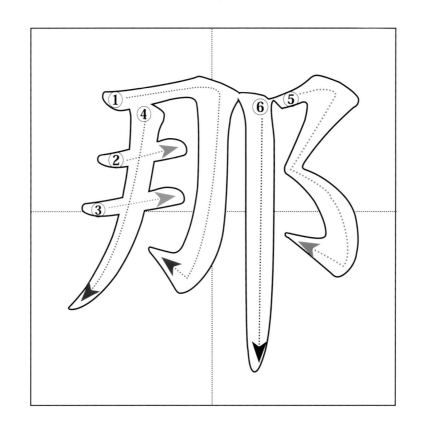

Lesson Two 第二課

nà

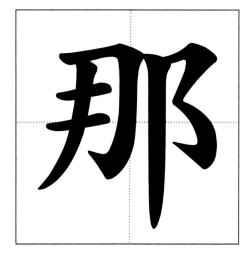

that

Nà shì shuí

那 是 誰 ？

Who is that?

The Stroke Orders 筆順

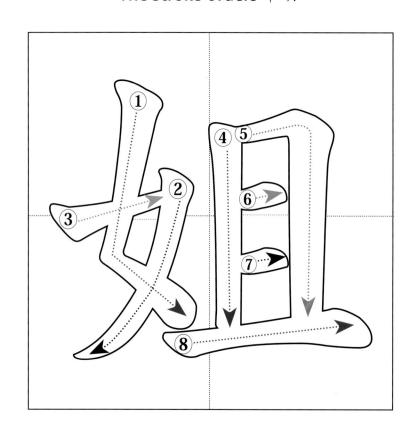

姐

elder sister

Nà shì wǒ jiě jie

那是我姐姐。

That is my elder sister.

The Stroke Orders 筆順

mèi

妹

younger sister

Mèi mei bǐ wǒ xiǎo

妹妹比我小。

妹妹 is younger than I am.

29

The Stroke Orders 筆順

zǐ

姊

elder sister

Wǒ yǒu zǐ mèi sān rén

我有姊妹三人。

I have two sisters.

The Stroke Orders 筆順

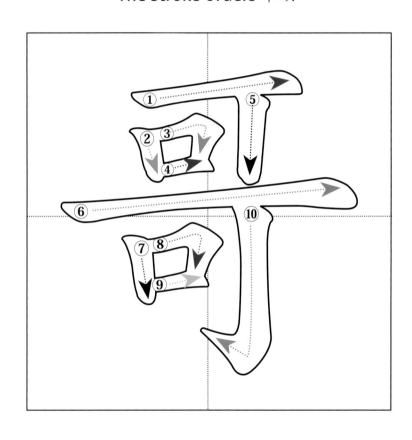

gē

elder brother

zhè shì wǒ gē ge

這是我哥哥。

This is my elder brother.

33

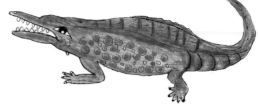

dà	ye/yé
大	爺

elder uncle

dà	mā
大	媽

elder aunt

gōng	gong
公	公

father-in-law

pó	po
婆	婆

mother-in-law

Yé ye shì shuí de bà ba
1. 爺爺是誰的爸爸？

Wài gōng shì shuí de bà ba
2. 外公是誰的爸爸？

Nǎi nai shì shuí de mā ma
3. 奶奶是誰的媽媽？

Wài pó shì shuí de mā ma
4. 外婆是誰的媽媽？

The Stroke Orders 筆順

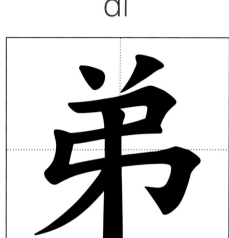

dì

弟

younger brother

Zhè shì wǒ dì di

這是我弟弟。

This is my younger brother.

The Stroke Orders 筆順

son/a suffix

Wǒ shì bà ba de ér zi

我是爸爸的兒子。

I am my father's son.

The Stroke Orders 筆順

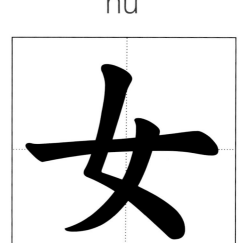

女

female

Wǒ shì mā ma de nǔ ér

我是媽媽的女兒。

I am my mother's daughter.

The Stroke Orders 筆順

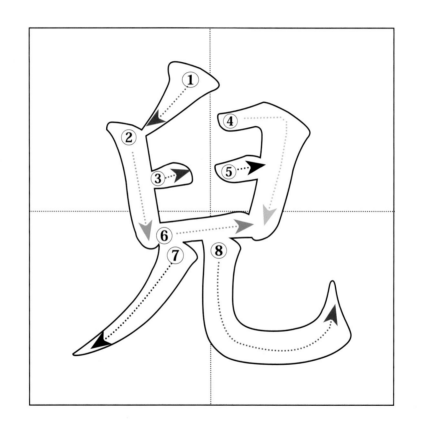

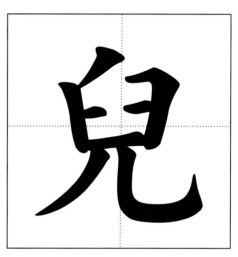

兒

son/a suffix

Er zi de ér zi shì sūn zi

兒子的兒子是孫子。

孫子 is one's son's son.

43

The Stroke Orders 筆順

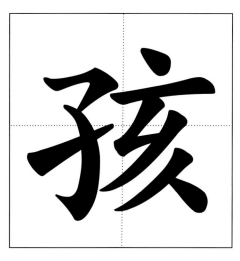

hái

children

Tā men shì nán háir

他們是男孩兒。

They are boys.

yé ye	wài gōng	bà ba	hái zi
爺爺	外公	爸爸	孩子
sūn zi	ér zi	nǚ ér	xiōng dì
孫子	兒子	女兒	兄弟
nǎi nai	mā ma	wài pó	dì mèi
奶奶	媽媽	外婆	弟妹

姊 姐 哪 第 弟 哥 那 妹

The Stroke Orders 筆順

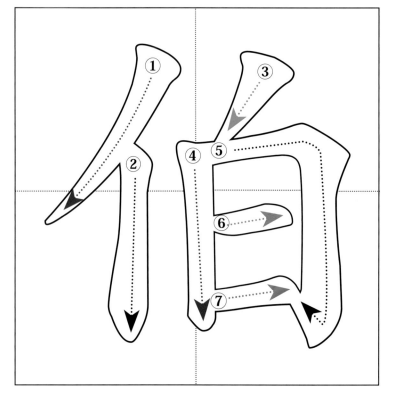

Lesson Three 第三課

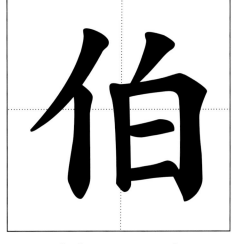

elder uncle
(on one's father's side)

Bó bo shì bà ba de gē ge
伯伯是爸爸的哥哥。
伯伯 is one's father's elder brother.

49

The Stroke Orders 筆順

gū

aunt
(on one's father's side)

Gū gu shì bà ba de jiě mèi

姑 姑 是 爸 爸 的 姐 妹。

姑姑 **is one's father's sister.**

The Stroke Orders 筆順

yí

aunt
(on one's mother's side)

Xiǎo yí shì mā mā de mèi mei

小姨是媽媽的妹妹。

小姨 is one's mother's younger sister.

53

The Stroke Orders 筆順

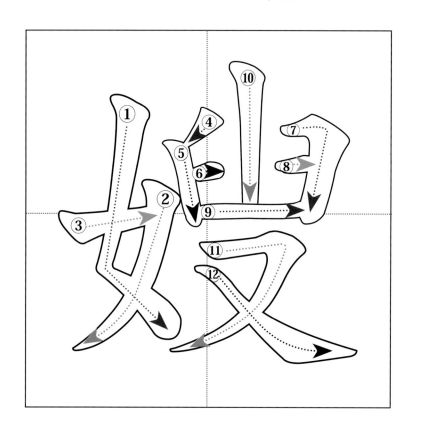

săo

sister-in-law
(elder brother's wife)

Săo zi shì gē gē de qī zi

嫂子是哥哥的妻子。

嫂子 is the wife of one's elder brother.

The Stroke Orders 筆順

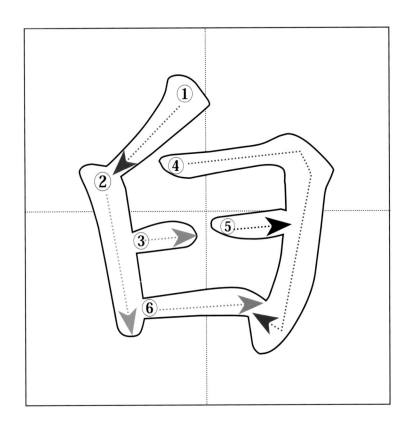

jiù

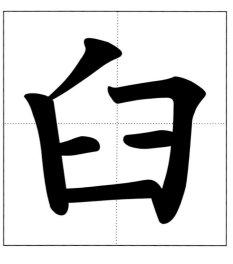

mortar/joint

Shí jiù shì gǔ dài rén yòng de
石臼是古代人用的。
Mortars are used by the ancient people.

57

shū

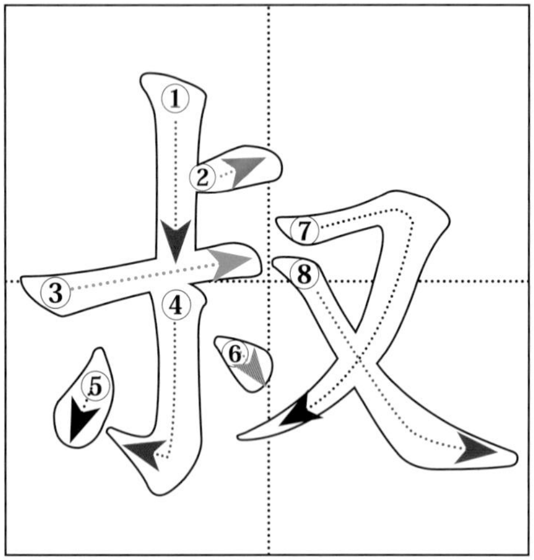

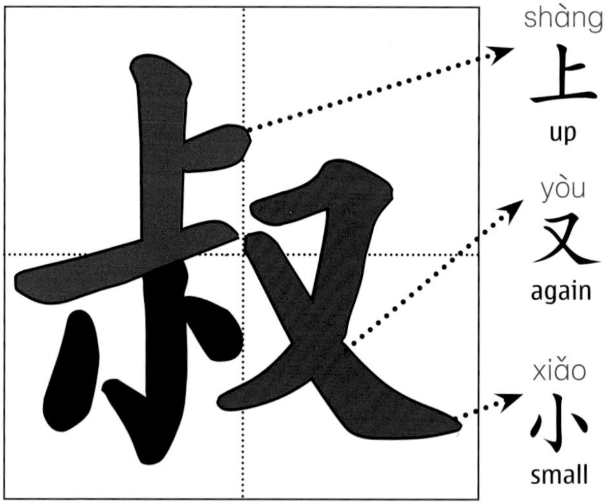

叔

shàng
上
up

yòu
又
again

xiǎo
小
small

younger uncle
(on one's father's side)

Shū shu shì bà ba de dì di
叔叔是爸爸的弟弟。
叔叔 is one's father's younger brother.

58

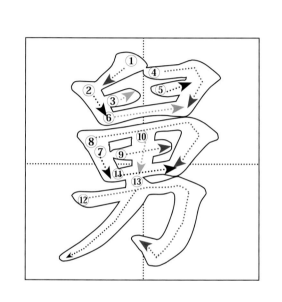

jiù

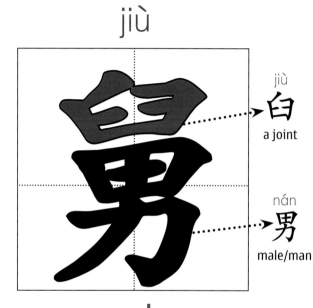

jiù
白
a joint

nán
男
male/man

uncle
(on one's mother's side)

Jiù jiu shì mā ma de xiōng dì*

舅 舅 是 媽 媽 的 兄 弟*。

舅舅 are one's mother's brothers.

*兄弟的「弟」泛指的時候輕讀。

jiù	mǔ
舅	母

aunt-in-law

bó	mǔ
伯	母

aunt-in-law

yí	fu
姨	夫

uncle-in-law

gū	fu
姑	父

uncle-in-law

jiě	fu
姐	夫

brother-in-law

mèi	fu
妹	夫

brother-in-law

dì	mèi
弟	妹

sister-in-law

sǎo	zi
嫂	子

sister-in-law

61

The Stroke Orders 筆順

niáng

娘

mum (dialect)

Tā shì Hánguó guó niang

她是韓國姑娘。

She is a Korean girl.

The Stroke Orders 筆順

yīng

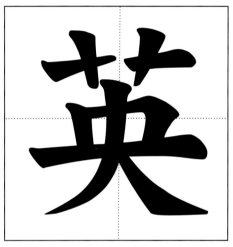

英

hero/English

Tā shì Yīngguó de xiǎo huǒ zi

他是英國的小夥子。

He is a young British man.

The Stroke Orders 筆順

媳

daughter-in-law/
wife

Tā de xí fù shì Fǎguórén

他的媳婦是法國人。

His wife is French.

The Stroke Orders 筆順

shěn

aunt *

Wǒ de shěn shen shì Xīnxīlánrén

我的嬸嬸是新西蘭人。

My aunt-in-law is a New Zealander.

* Younger uncle's wife on one's father's side. 叔叔的妻子。

The Stroke Orders 筆順

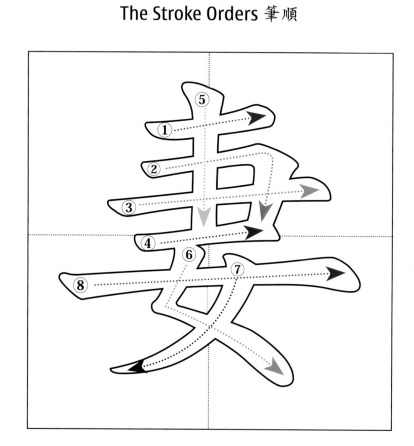

wife (formal)

Tā de qī zi shì Rìběnrén

他的妻子是日本人。

His wife is a Japanese lady.

71

lǎo	gōng
老	公

hubby (colloquial)

lǎo	po
老	婆

wife (colloquial)

ài	ren
愛	人

husband/wife/lover

fū	qī
夫	妻

married couple

Match the characters with the cartoons.
字畫相配。

爸 娘 浪 英 媳 伯 拍 姨

The Stroke Orders 筆順

Lesson Four 第四課

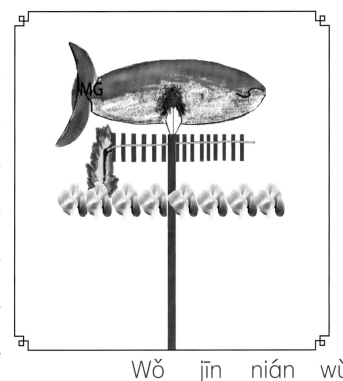

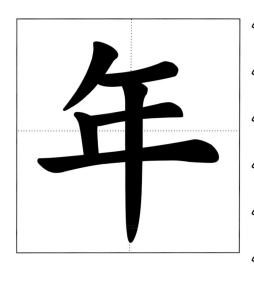

nián

年

year

Wǒ jīn nián wǔ suì

我今年五歲。

I am five years old (this year).

The Stroke Orders 筆順

surname

Wǒ xìng wáng
我 姓 王 。
My surname is Wang.

The Stroke Orders 筆順

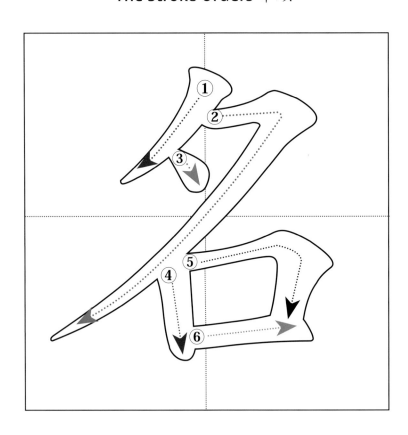

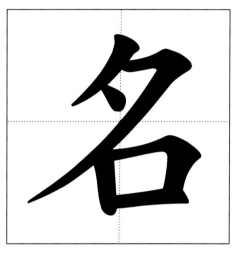

first name

Wǒ de míng zi shì Wáng Yù

我 的 名 字 是 王 玉 。

My name is Wang Yu.

79

The Stroke Orders 筆順

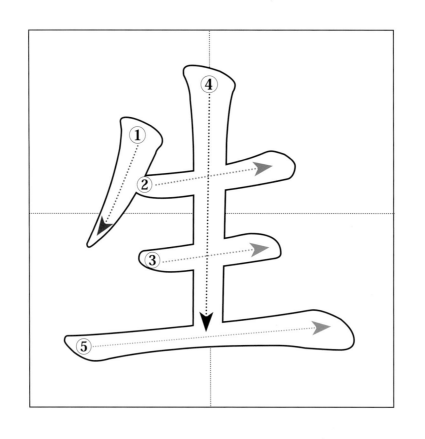

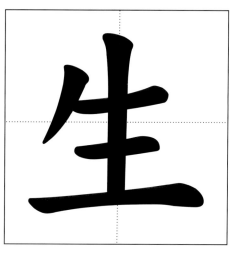

bear/born

jīn tiān shì wǒ de shēng rì

今天是我的生日。

Today is my birthday.

87

The Stroke Orders 筆順

nǎ

哪

where

Nín de shēng rì shì nǎ yì tiān

您的生日是哪一天？

Which day is your birthday?

83

Nǐ jǐ suì le
1. 你幾歲了？
How old are you?

Nǐ xìng shén me
2. 你姓甚麼？
How old will you be next year?

Nǐ jiào shén me míng zi
3. 你叫甚麼名字？
What's your name?

Nǐ zhù zài nǎ lǐ
4. 你住在哪裡？
Where do you live?

Nǐ shì nǎ guó rén
5. 你是哪國人？
What nationality are you?

shén | me
甚 | 麼
what

nǚ

女

female/woman

nán

男

male/man

nǚ	shēng
女	生

female student

nán	shēng
男	生

male student

nǚ	cè	suǒ
女	廁	所

ladies' room

nán	cè	suǒ
男	廁	所

men's room

The Stroke Orders 筆順

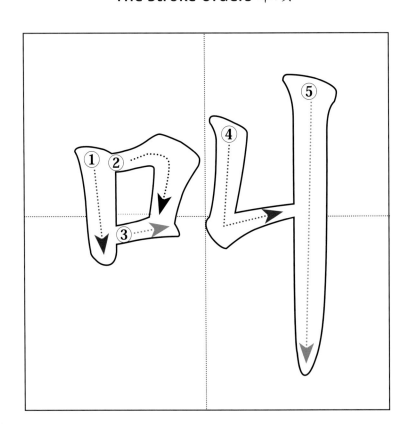

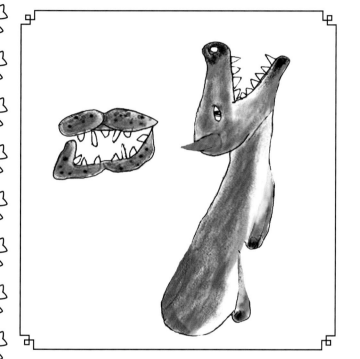

jiào

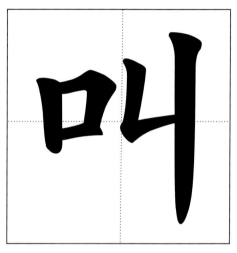

howl/call/yell

Wǒ de gǒu jiào Xiǎo Máo

我的狗叫小毛。

My dog is called Xiao Mao.

The Stroke Orders 筆順

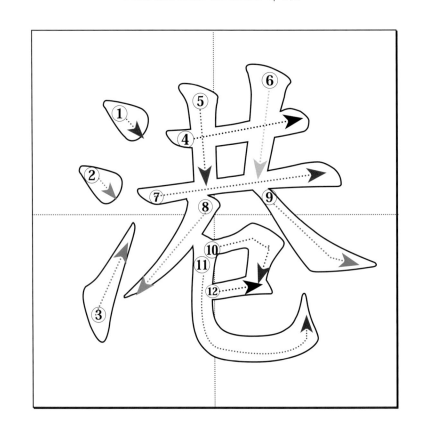

port

Wǒ shì Xiānggǎngrén

我是香港人。

I am a Hong Kong man.

89

The Stroke Orders 筆順

dū/dōu

都

capital/a surname

tā men dōu shì Zhōngguórén
他們都是中國人。

They are all Chinese.

The Stroke Orders 筆順

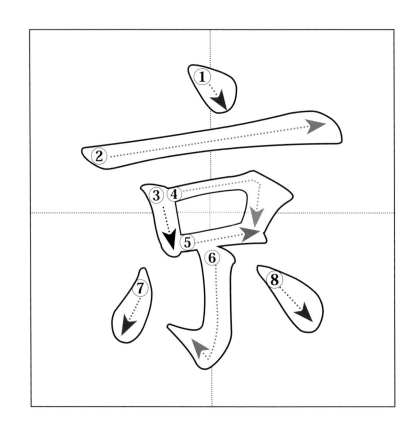

the capital

Wǒ de lǎo jiā zài Běijīng
我的老家在北京。
Beijing is my hometown.

The Stroke Orders 筆順

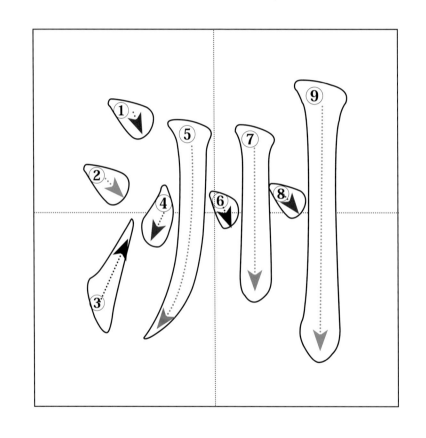

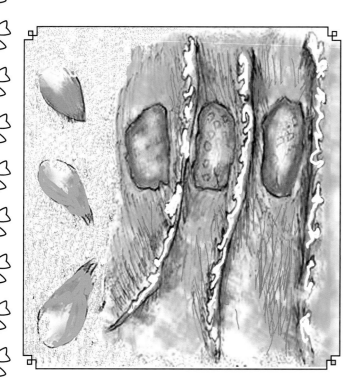

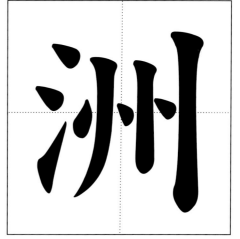

continent

Wǒ zhù zài Àozhōu

我 住 在 澳 洲 。

I am an Australian.

bú shì

不是

be not

tā bú shì wǒ gē ge
他不是我哥哥。
He is not my elder brother.

tā bú shì wǒ mèi mei
她不是我妹妹。
She is not my younger sister.

tā bú shì wǒ shū shu
他不是我叔叔。
He is not my younger uncle.

méi yǒu

沒有

have no/have none

wǒ méi yǒu gē ge
我沒有哥哥。
I have no elder brothers.

wǒ méi yǒu mèi mei
我沒有妹妹。
I have no younger sisters.

wǒ méi yǒu shū shu
我沒有叔叔。
I have no younger uncles.

Wǒ jiào Wáng Xiǎo É， wǒ jiā yǒu bā kǒu
我叫王小娥，我家有八口

rén。 Tā men shì bà ba、 mā ma、 yé
人。他們是爸爸、媽媽、爺

ye hé nǎi nai。 Wǒ yǒu yí gè jiě jie、
爺和奶奶。我有一個姐姐、

liǎng gè gē ge。 Wǒ hái yǒu dà yí、 xiǎo
兩個哥哥。我還有大姨、小

yí、 dà bó、 shū shu hé xiǎo gū。
姨、大伯、叔叔和小姑。

97

Zhōng	guó
中	國

China

Yīng	guó
英	國

England

Měi	guó
美	國

U.S.A

Fǎ	guó
法	國

France

Dé	guó
德	國

Germany

Stickers

小貼紙

99

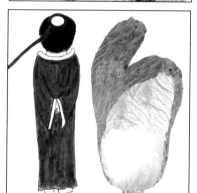

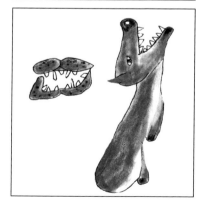
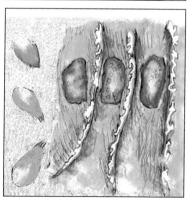

103

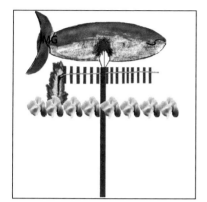

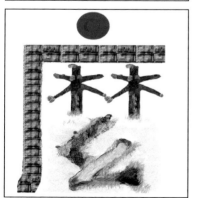

104

mā 媽	bà 爸	gē 哥
媽	爸	哥

jiě 姐	mèi 妹	dì 弟
姐	妹	弟

nǎi 奶	tā 牠	bó 伯
奶	牠	伯
shěn 嬸	shū 叔	jiě/zǐ 姊
嬸	叔	姊

pó 婆	gǎng 港	jiù 臼
婆	港	臼

yí 姨	xí 媳	qī 妻
姨	媳	妻

dū/dōu 都	nǔ 女	hái 孩
都	女	孩
niáng 娘	sǎo 嫂	jiē 節
娘	嫂	節

yīng 英	tā 她	tā 他
英		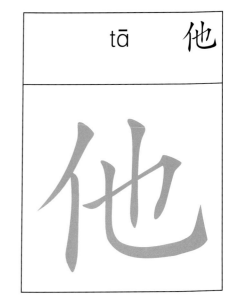

wǒ 我	nǐ 你	gū 姑
我		

jiào 叫	shēng 生	xìng 姓
叫	生	姓

nián 年	míng 名	shì 是
年	名	是

de 的	jīng 京	shén 甚
的	京	甚

nà 那	nǎ 哪	zhōu 洲
那	哪	洲

jiù 舅	yǒu 有	ér 兒
	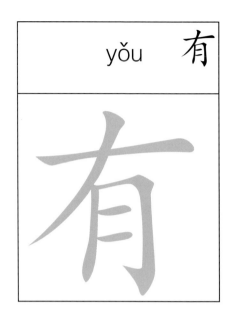	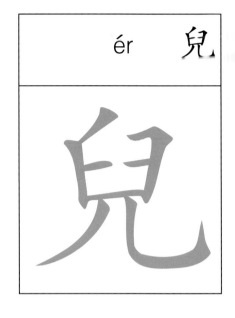

zǐ 子	me 麼	shuí 誰
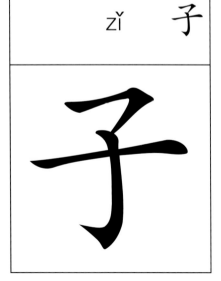		

Vocabulary
詞彙

1. 我　I/me
2. 是　be/is/am/are
3. 娥　a girl's name
4. 她　she/her
5. 誰　who
6. 媽　mother
7. 他　he/him
8. 爸　father
9. 你　you
10. 你好　how are you
11. 爺　grandpa
12. 不是　be not
13. 奶　grandma/milk
14. 公　male/public
15. 外公　grandfather
　　(on one's mother's side)
16. 婆　old lady
17. 外婆　grandmother
　　(on one's mother's side)
18. 的　of
19. 白菜　cabbage
20. 做的　be made of
21. 姥爺　grandpa
　　(on one's mother's side)
22. 姥姥　grandma
　　(on one's mother's side)
23. 父親　father
24. 母親　mother

25. 那　that
26. 姐　elder sister
27. 妹　younger sister
28. 比……小　younger than
29. 姊　elder sister
30. 姊妹　sisters
31. 哥　elder brother
32. 大爺　elder uncle
33. 大媽　elder aunt
34. 公公　father-in-law
35. 婆婆　mother-in-law
36. 這是　this is
37. 弟　younger brother
38. 子　son/suffix
39. 兒子　son
40. 女　female
41. 女兒　daughter
42. 兒　son
43. 孫子　grandson
44. 孩　children
45. 他們　they
46. 男孩兒　boy
47. 弟妹　sister-in-law
48. 兄弟　brothers
49. 伯　elder uncle
　　(on one's father's side)
50. 姑　aunt
　　(on one's father's side)

51. 姐妹　sisters
52. 小姨　younger aunt
　　(on one's mother's side)
53. 嫂　sister-in-law
54. 嫂子　sister-in-law
55. 妻子　wife
56. 白　mortar/joint
57. 石白　stone mortar
58. 古代人　ancient people
59. 使用的　used
60. 叔　younger uncle
　　(on one's father's side)
61. 舅　younger uncle
　　(on one's mother's side)
62. 舅母　aunt-in-law
　　(on one's mother's side)
63. 伯母　aunt-in-law
　　(on one's father's side)
64. 姨夫　uncle-in-law
　　(on one's mother's side)
65. 姑父　uncle-in-law
　　(on one's father's side)
66. 姐夫　brother-in-law
67. 妹夫　brother-in-law
68. 娘　mother (dialect)
69. 韓國　South Korea
70. 姑娘　girl
71. 英　hero/handsome

#	漢字	English	#	漢字	English
72.	英國	Britain/England	101.	甚麼	what
73.	小夥子	young man	102.	男	male
74.	媳	daughter-in-law/wife	103.	女生	female student
75.	媳婦	wife	104.	男生	male student
76.	法國人	French	105.	中國人	Chinese
77.	嬸	aunt-in-law	106.	女廁所	ladies' room
78.	嬸嬸	aunt-in-law (on one's father's side)	107.	男廁所	men's room
79.	新西蘭人	New Zealander	108.	叫	howl/call/yell
			109.	港	port
80.	妻	wife	110.	香港人	Hong Kong people
81.	日本人	Japanese	111.	都	all/capital
82.	老公	buddy (colloquial)	112.	京	the capital
83.	老婆	wife (colloquial)	113.	老家	birthplace
84.	愛人	title for husband/wife	114.	北京	Beijing
85.	夫妻	married couple	115.	洲	continent
86.	今年	this year	116.	澳洲	Australia
87.	五歲	five years old	117.	沒有	have no
88.	歲	years old	118.	美国	U.S.A
89.	姓	family name	119.	法国	France
90.	王	king/a surname	120.	德国	Germany
91.	名	first name			
92.	名字	name			
93.	生	bear/born			
94.	今天	today			
95.	生日	birthday			
96.	哪	where/which			
97.	幾歲	how old			
98.	住在	live			
99.	哪裡	where			
100.	哪國人	what nationality			